Adventures in the Castle

By

Beaver Street Kindergarten Red Group

ISBN-13: 978-1722391607

ISBN-10: 172239160X

Pages

Jane
Tess
Lucas
Laura
Billy
Alannah S
Wolfgang
Alannah B
Ryan
Cordelia
Oscar
Piper
Oliver
Emma
Jamieson
Amy
Nam
Lucy
Luca
Elani
Nate
Chloe
Elliot
Tamsin
Aston
Olivia
Reanne
Roslyn
Melissa
Carina
Frances

Once upon a time a boy and girl found a castle.

They go in the castle and play.

Then they hurt themselves,
the shield protected them
from the monster with big
legs.

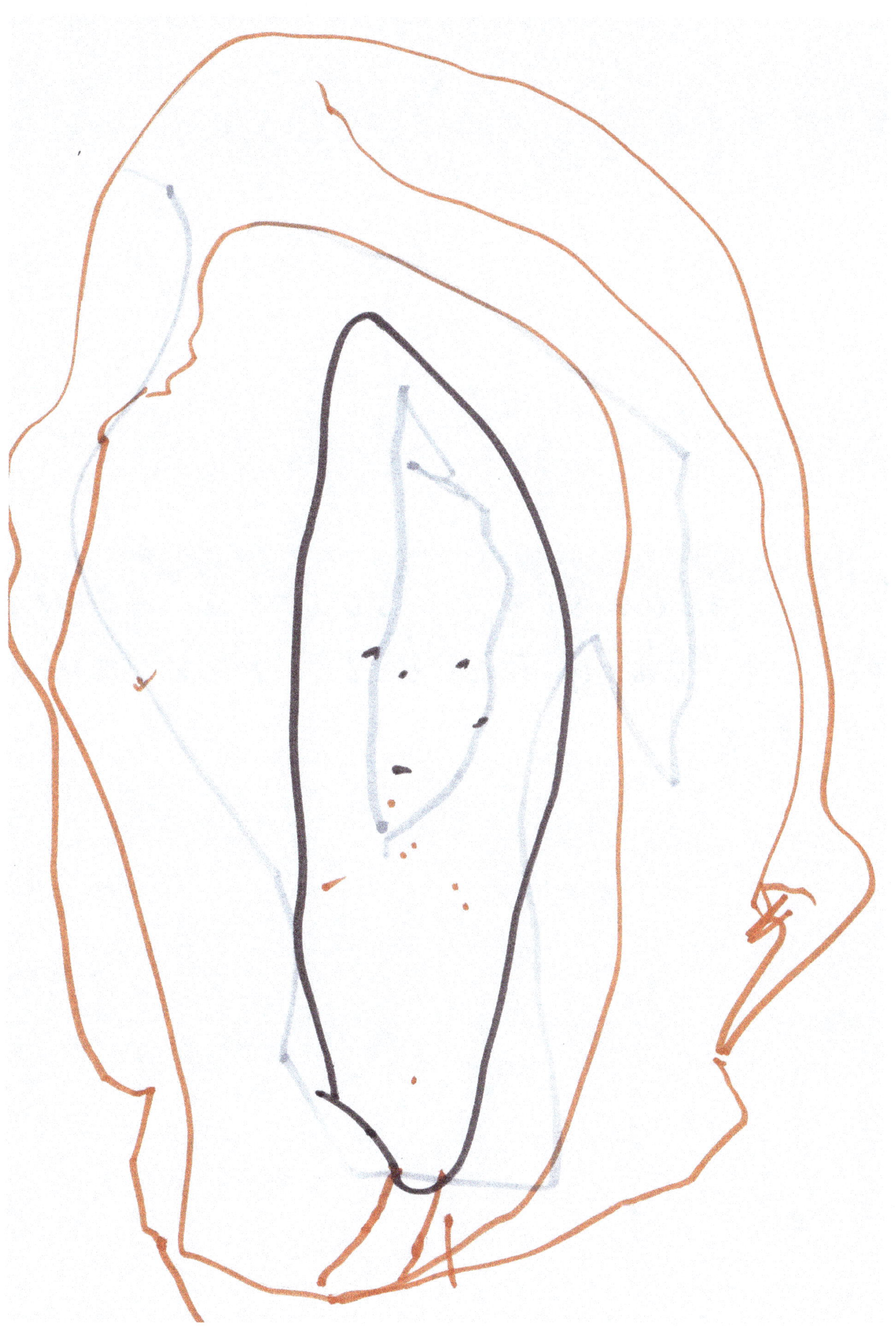

The monster scared them away. they have to run away faster.

They come back to the castle
in the rain.

They find another castle.

They throw away a TV, there is a bed, a table, and a circle in the room.

A policeman gets some bad guys. he puts the bad guys in jail.

The truck runs them over.

A unicorn is sniffing some flowers.

They get the TV again and they watch the TV.

They drive the car, they go back home.

A butterfly appears, they jump on the butterfly and fly back to the castle. The monster is sleeping so they tiptoe. Then a gingerbread man came and a balloon appears. It can talk. There is a stick and a water bottle, they drink the water but there was someone inside. A genie, and they turned into a genie. Then the stick pops the balloon but the balloon keeps reappearing. The boy laughs but when you laugh you go on the roof. And then everything is gone and they wake up from sleeping, it was a dream and they tell their mum about their dream. Their house could walk and it looked like a piggy bank but it was actually a talking pig with a roof on it.

A boy and a girl find a castle. they find a tree and a treasure box.

A lizard is walking on its two tipytoes, they find a big Charizard dragon.

The monster comes again. it tries to chase them. it wants to eat them.

The monster comes in the jail and the butterfly brings them to the police. The volcano monster put lava over everything.

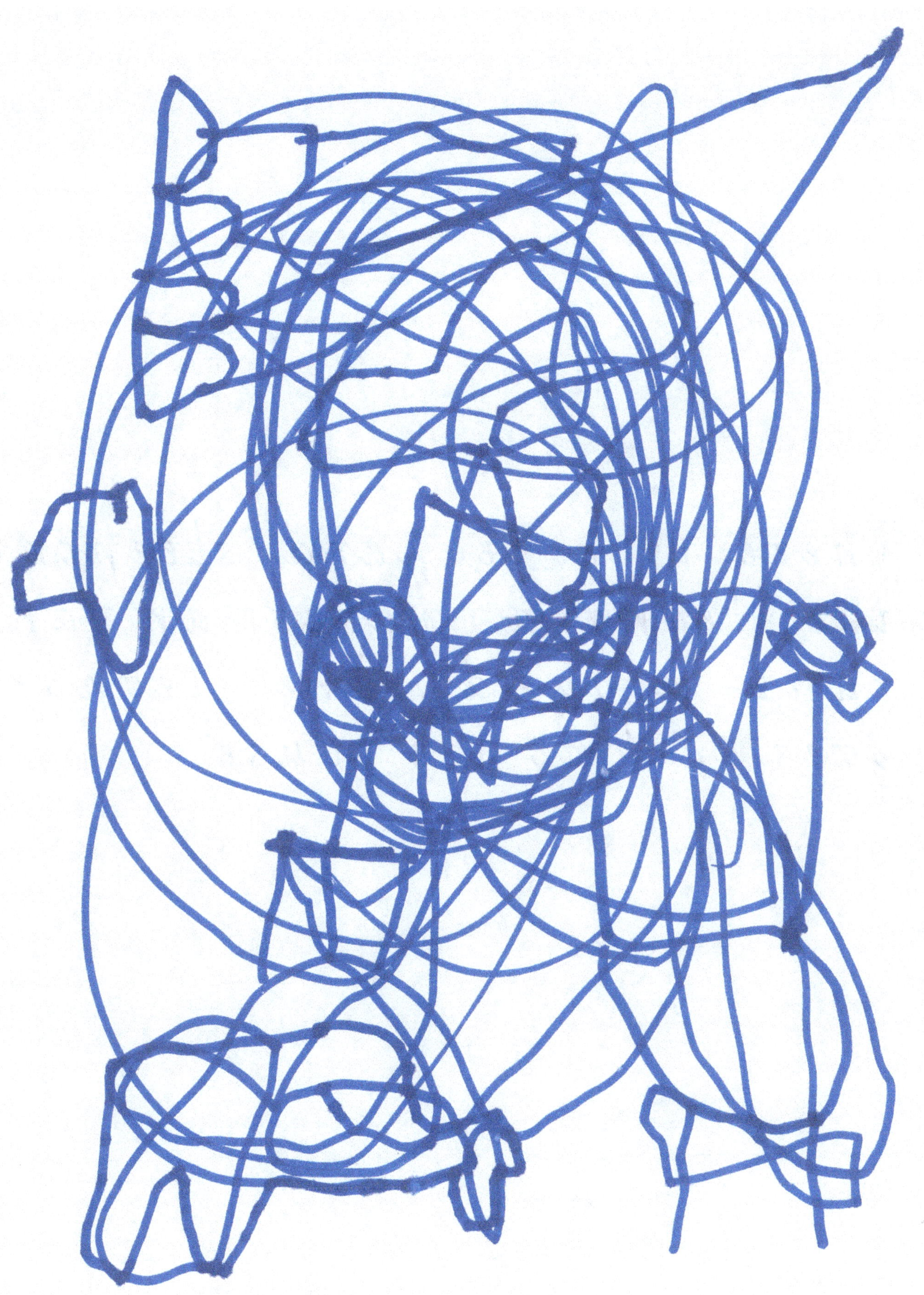

There is a leopard sleeping.
the leopard wakes up and
runs around. The leopard
goes back to its house.

The bad guys go in jail.

A unicorn coming to save the good guys who are in jail. and the goodies are saying you can't save them.

There is a dinosaur walking,
there is a dinosaur sleeping
and it wakes up. The
princess runs away from the
T-Rex.

They get the TV back, they're watching Peter Rabbit.

Dinosaurs crossing the jungle.

Then the person saw the tiger and the trees.

They cut some wood off. they get the TV and bring it to the camp spot.

A girl and boy watching TV
in their castle.

A magic bee appears in front of the TV.

It buzzes and buzzes and buzzes and lands on top of the table.

The boy and girl were scared of the bee and opened the door to let it out.

After the bee was let out the cat spotted it in the yard and tried to chase it.

The bee spotted the bee hotel
in the garden and went in
for a safe place to stay.